I AM READING

Alien Alby

KAYE U

Illustr

SOPHIE ROHRBACH

MACMILLAN CHILDREN'S BOOKS

For Mo and Ella

First published 2009 by Macmillan Children's Books
a division of Macmillan Publishers Limited
20 New Wharf Road, London N1 9RR
Basingstoke and Oxford
Associated companies throughout the world
www.panmacmillan.com

ISBN 978-0-330-51013-4

1 3 5 7 9 8 6 4 2

A CIP catalogue record for this book is available from
the British Library.

Printed in China

Contents

Chapter One

4

Chapter Two

9

Chapter Three

18

Chapter Four

22

Chapter Five

28

Chapter Six

35

Chapter One

Alby was an Alien. Sometimes he looked like this . . .

But usually he looked like this.

Alby lived on an Alien planet.

He had a mum, a dad and a sister
called Arlene. Here they are, smiling.
Well, Arlene isn't.

Alby had a faithful Squeeble called Squee. Squeebles are popular Alien pets. They are orange and happy. They bounce and knock things over.

Sometimes Squee looked like this . . .

And sometimes like this.

Home was a Dome. It looked like this on the outside . . .

And this on the inside.

The Dome was very tidy. Alby's mum was fussy.

The garden was tidy too. Well, the bits you could see. There was a weedy, swampy bit, but that was hidden behind the bushes.

Alby and Squee weren't allowed to play there.

Keep out! That means YOU Alby! mum

They did though.

Chapter Two

Alby's room wasn't tidy. It was bursting with noisy Alien toys. Most of them went BOING! BANG! POP! and WHEEEE!

He had a Groobleblaster

and a Splattermerang.

He had a Swizzelwizzel,

a Nargian Nose Flute

and a Zoomeroo.

He ate tons of Alien cereal and sent off for free stuff. He had hundreds of Alien Animal stickers that he never got round to sticking. He had a huge collection of Space Warriors, mostly in bits, because Squee liked chewing them.

He saved up and ordered a Wombian Wobble Board from a catalogue.

He hurt himself on that one.

Alby had quiet things too, which he kept for night-time: his books and his toy catalogues and his old cuddly toys. His favourite was the purple thing with three heads, called Purpy.

Alby slept with Purpy. And Squee, of
course. He always slept with Squee.

13

Alby had a favourite story called *Planet of the Earthlings.* It was all about funny-looking creatures who liked food called "Chips". They had pets called "Dogs" and they slept with things called "Teddies".

Alby's mum wasn't happy with Alby's
toy collection. She called it a load of old
rubbish. Sometimes she threw things out,
which made Alby cry all night.

Most of Alby's games required a lot of running around, so his mum made him play outside.

He played with the Zoomeroo until it broke.

He squirted Squee with the Splattermerang.

He Groobleblasted
Squee too! That
was fun! Then
they ran around
again.

Somehow they ended up in the muddy
bit of garden where they weren't
allowed. And that's how the trouble
started.

Chapter Three

"What's this on the carpet?" said Alby's mum. "It's mud, isn't it?"

"Is it?" said Alby.

"Yes. And you know how it got there, don't you?"

"Do I?"

"Yes. You brought it in. You and Squee."

"I wiped my feet," said Alby.

"Squee didn't though, did he? You're supposed to remind him. He's your responsibility. You've been down at the swamp again, haven't you? What have I said about that?"

"We just sort of fell there by accident."

"Well, you can get those marks out, then go to your room. And take Squee with you."

It took ages to clean the carpet. Alby's mum nagged and Squee sat in a corner, looking small and sad.

Then Alby went to his room.

"This is all your fault," he grumbled. "I keep telling you to wipe your feet."

He did. But Squee always forgot. He was a Squeeble. They are good at playing and squealing, but they have terrible memories.

Chapter Four

It wouldn't have been so bad if it hadn't

happened again the next day. They

shouldn't have gone to the swampy bit,

of course, but it had been raining in the
night. Alien rain makes great mud for
sliding.

This time, cleaning the carpet took even longer. Squee was put outside in disgrace.

He was still there at teatime.

For tea they had Woodlydoodlynoodly Strings. They ate them using fiddle sticks, which are like revolving prongs.

But Alby wasn't hungry.

"Can't he come in now?" he asked.

"Eat your Strings," said his mum. "You too, Arlene."

"I don't like Woodlydoodlynoodly Strings," said Arlene. "I want food that sounds shorter."

"Like Chips," said Alby. "That's what they eat in *Planet of the Earthlings.*"

"You'll eat what you're given," said his mum. "Ah, here's your dad."

In came Alby's dad with something in his arms.

"Right," he said, dumping it on the table. "This should do the trick."

Oh! Oh *no*!

It was a Squeeble Dome!

"I hope that's not for Squee," said Alby.

But it was. Even Arlene was shocked.

"We warned you enough times," said Alby's mum.

"But he always sleeps with me!"

"Not any more," said his dad. "He's got his own Dome now. He'll love it."

Chapter Five

But Squee didn't love his Dome. He
hated it. It was small and draughty.
Worst of all, it was far away from Alby.
"You'll be all right," said Alby. "I'll
bring you some supper."

Squee licked Alby's knee and said,
"Squee." But there wasn't any joy in it.
And he didn't want any supper.
"I know," said Alby. "I'll bring out the
Splattermerang. You like that, don't you?"

29

But Squee wasn't interested in the Splattermerang. Or the Swizzelwizzel. He didn't even cheer up when Alby played him a tune on the Nargian Nose Flute.

"Stop making that racket and come on in," shouted Alby's mum. "It's bedtime!"

"You'll be all right," said Alby again. "I've got to go now."

And he collected up all the unwanted toys and went inside to bed.

He didn't sleep though. He lay hugging Purpy, thinking about poor little Squee outside, all on his own in the night, with nothing to comfort him. Whatever could he do?

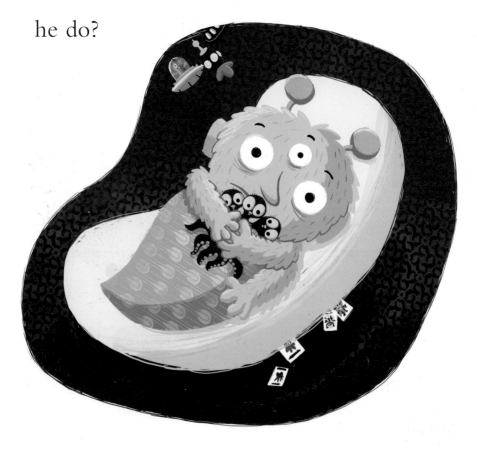

Squee shivered in his Dome. It was raining again. He wished he was in Alby's room, on Alby's bed. Why was he here? He didn't know. He was only a Squeeble.

His fur pricked up when he heard a footstep. Then he smelt a familiar smell.

"Here," whispered Alby. "Have him. See you in the morning."

It was Purpy. Purpy smelt of Alby.

It wasn't perfect, but it was the next best thing. Both of them slept quite well in the end.

Chapter Six

Next morning Alby and Squee were on their very best behaviour. Squee didn't break anything and neither of them went near any mud. In the afternoon they sat in the garden reading *Planet of the Earthlings*.

Later, Alby looked at a new catalogue
that had just arrived. There was
something really good in it! Something
very expensive, but great!

That night, Squee slept in his Dome again,
but he had Purpy, so it wasn't too bad.

Alby lay in bed, planning.

The following day, Alby's mum let him
hold a Grand Toy Sale outside the gate.

He sold the
Groobleblaster,

the Splattermerang and the Wombian
Wobble Board. He
sold the
Swizzelwizzel
and the
Nargian Nose

Flute. He gave
away the broken Zoomeroo. He got rid
of the chewed-up Space Warriors.

Nobody wanted the stickers, so he was
stuck with them. He sold everything
except Purpy.

There still wasn't quite enough money, but
Arlene chipped in, which was nice of her.
Then Alby sent off for . . .

. . . a *Luxury Squeeble Feet Cleaner!*
It was fully automated, with little
revolving brushes. Here it is, right by
the back door:

Squee loved the Feet Cleaner, because it
tickled. He never once forgot to use it.

In the end, he was allowed back indoors to sleep with Alby – and Purpy, of course.

They didn't need the Squeeble Dome
any more, so Alby's mum made his dad
throw it behind the bushes in the
swampy bit, where Alby and Squee
weren't allowed to go.

They sometimes did though!

About the Author and Illustrator

Kaye Umansky was born in Devon and came to London to be a teacher. She has been writing children's books for twenty-one years. She has a husband, a grown-up daughter, two cats and thirteen fish in a tank. She likes to read funny books. 'I wish I had a Squeeble for a pet,' says Kaye, 'but I don't think my cats would like it.'

Sophie Rohrbach was born in Strasbourg, France. She studied illustration in Lyon, where she now lives with her darling, her daughter and her brushes. Sophie is passionate about the colours and patterns that she uses in her illustrations. She loves to include details in her pictures to achieve small worlds full of fantasy and colour.

Tips for Beginner Readers

1. Think about the cover and the title of the book. What do you think it will be about? While you are reading, think about what might happen next and why.

2. As you read, ask yourself if what you're reading makes sense. If it doesn't, try rereading or look at the pictures for clues.

3. If there is a word that you do not know, look carefully at the letters, sounds and word parts that you do know. Blend the sounds to read the word. Is this a word you know? Does it make sense in the sentence?

4. Think about the characters, where the story takes place, and the problems the characters in the story faced. What are the important ideas in the beginning, middle and end of the story?

5. Ask yourself questions like:
Did you like the story?
Why or why not?
How did the author make it fun to read?
How well did you understand it?

Maybe you can understand the story you read it again!

About the Author and Illustrator

Kaye Umansky was born in Devon and came to London to be a teacher. She has been writing children's books for twenty-one years. She has a husband, a grown-up daughter, two cats and thirteen fish in a tank. She likes to read funny books.
'I wish I had a Squeeble for a pet,' says Kaye, 'but I don't think my cats would like it.'

Sophie Rohrbach was born in Strasbourg, France. She studied illustration in Lyon, where she now lives with her darling, her daughter and her brushes. Sophie is passionate about the colours and patterns that she uses in her illustrations. She loves to include details in her pictures to achieve small worlds full of fantasy and colour.

Tips for Beginner Readers

1. Think about the cover and the title of the book. What do you think it will be about? While you are reading, think about what might happen next and why.

2. As you read, ask yourself if what you're reading makes sense. If it doesn't, try rereading or look at the pictures for clues.

3. If there is a word that you do not know, look carefully at the letters, sounds and word parts that you do know. Blend the sounds to read the word. Is this a word you know? Does it make sense in the sentence?

4. Think about the characters, where the story takes place, and the problems the characters in the story faced. What are the important ideas in the beginning, middle and end of the story?

5. Ask yourself questions like:
Did you like the story?
Why or why not?
How did the author make it fun to read?
How well did you understand it?

Maybe you can understand the story better if you read it again!